HOW BIG? HOW FAST? HOW HUNGRY?

A Book About Cats

Thanks to the Scientists' Institute for Public Information and S. Barbara Dashow, M.S.C.D.E., for help with this book.

Photos: Pages 6–7 Tom McHugh/Photo Researchers; pages 10–11 Terry Murphy/Animals Animals; pages 14–15 E.R. Degginger/Animals Animals; page 18 (T) Tom McHugh/Photo Researchers; page 18 (B) Terry Murphy/Animals Animals; page 19 E.R. Degginger/Animals Animals; pages 20–21 Michael & Barbara Reed/Animals Animals

Library of Congress number: 90-8026

Library of Congress Cataloging in Publication Data

Waverly, Barney.
  How big? how fast? how hungry?: a book about cats / by Barney Waverly; illustrated by Steve Henry.
  (Ready-set-read)
  Summary: Uses humorous illustrations to compare the traits and habits of domestic cats with those of lions, tigers, and cheetahs that live in the wild.
  1. Cats—Juvenile literature. 2. Felidae—Juvenile literature. [1. Cats. 2. Felidae.] I. Henry, Steve, ill. II. Title. III. Series.
SF445.7.W39 1990   599.74'428—dc20   90-8026
ISBN 0-8172-3582-5

1 2 3 4 5 6 7 8 9   94 93 92 91 90

READY·SET·READ

How Big? How Fast? How Hungry?

A Book About Cats

by Barney Waverly

illustrated by Steve Henry

Raintree Publishers

Milwaukee

4

When you think of a cat,
you probably think of a house cat.

But . . .

5

A tiger is also a cat.
A tiger is much bigger than a house cat.
A tiger is the biggest cat there is.

How big is a tiger?

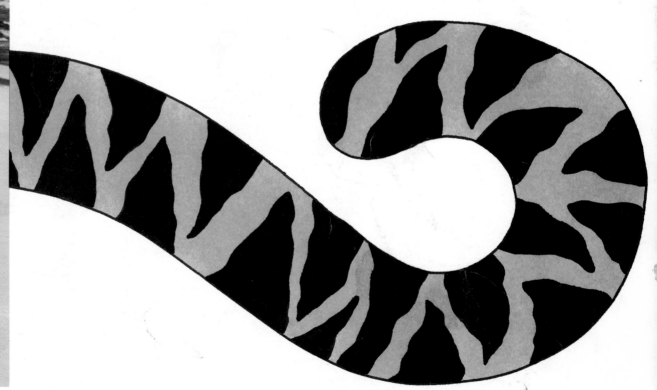

This **BIG!**

If you weighed a tiger, you'd find that
it weighs about 600 pounds.

8

If you weighed a house cat, you'd find that
it weighs about 8 pounds.

9

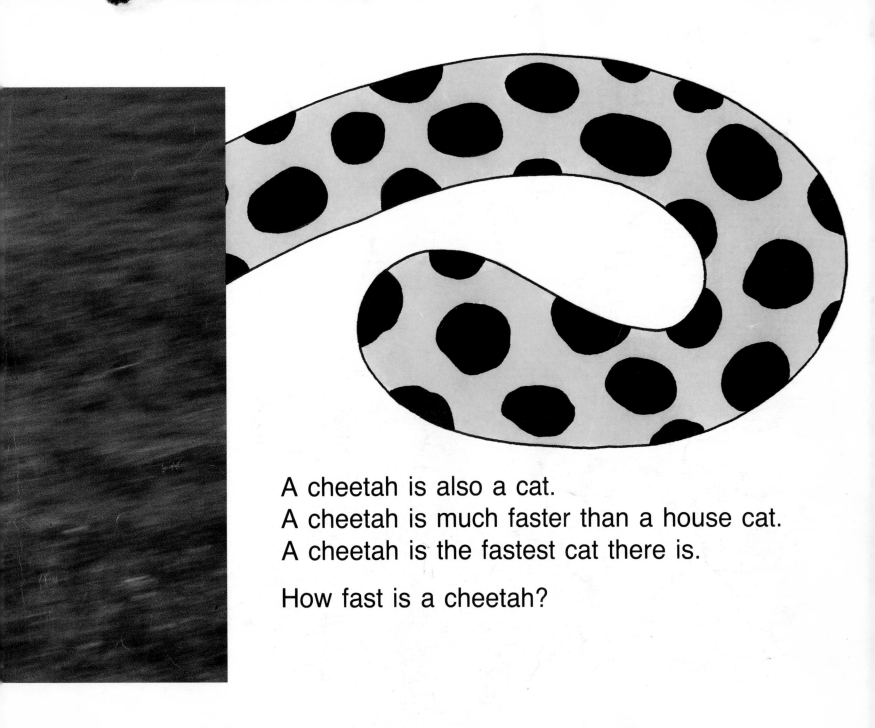

A cheetah is also a cat.
A cheetah is much faster than a house cat.
A cheetah is the fastest cat there is.

How fast is a cheetah?

This **FAST!**

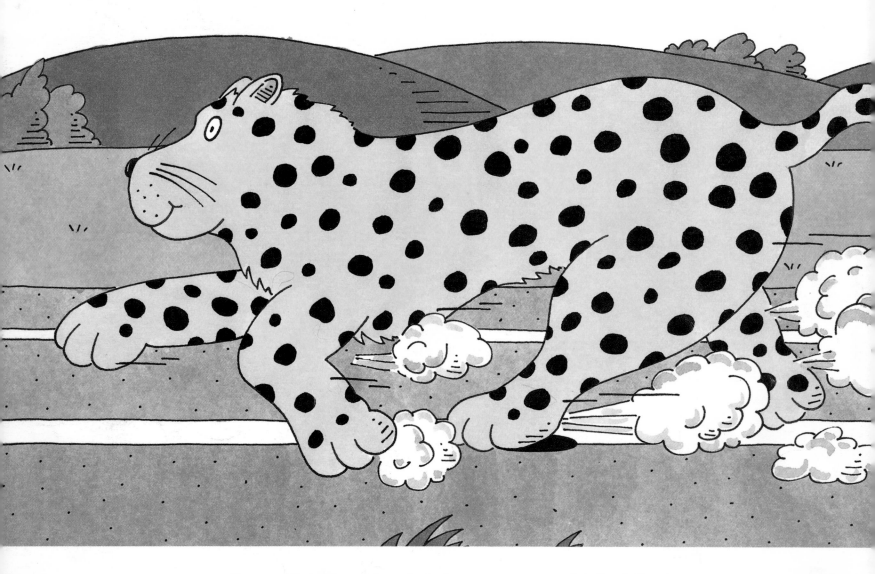

If you timed a cheetah in a race, you'd find that
it can run 70 miles an hour.

If you timed a house cat in a race, you'd find that
it can run 30 miles an hour.

A lion is also a cat.
A lion is much hungrier than a house cat.
A lion is the hungriest cat there is.

How hungry is a lion?

This **HUNGRY!**

If you fed a lion, you'd find that
it eats about 75 pounds of meat.

16

If you fed a house cat, you'd find that
it eats about $\frac{1}{5}$ pound of meat.

A tiger is the biggest cat.

A cheetah is the fastest cat.

18

A lion is the hungriest cat.

They are all wild cats.

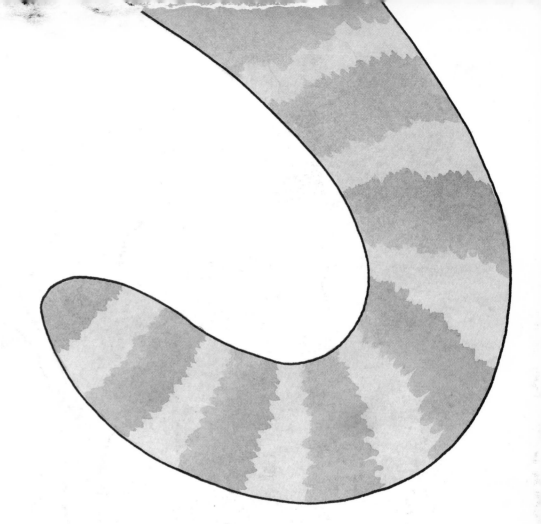

A house cat is not wild.
A house cat is tame.
A house cat is cuddly—

The only cuddly cat there is!

23

Sharing the Joy of Reading

Reading a book aloud to your child is just one way you can help your child experience the joy of reading. Now that you and your child have shared **How Big? How Fast? How Hungry?,** you can help your child begin to think and react as a reader by encouraging him or her to:

- Retell or reread the story with you, looking and listening for the repetition of specific letters, sounds, words, or phrases.

- Make a picture of a favorite character, event, or key concept from this book.

- Talk about his or her own ideas and feelings about the subject of this book and other things he or she might want to know about this subject.

Here is an activity that you can do together to help extend your child's appreciation of this book: You and your child can play an animal word game. In **How Big? How Fast? How Hungry?,** a cat is described as "cuddly" and a lion is described as "hungry." Take turns with your child naming an animal and then coming up with a word that describes that animal.